50p childrens

childrens

(53)

THE GIGGLER TREATMENT

Look out for Roddy Doyle's
other fantastic children's books:

ROVER SAVES CHRISTMAS
THE MEANWHILE ADVENTURES
WILDERNESS

Roddy Doyle

The giggler Treatment

Illustrated by Brian Ajhar

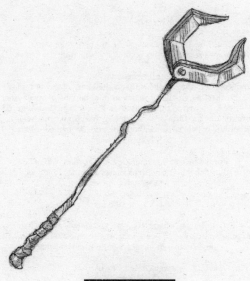

■ SCHOLASTIC

Scholastic Children's Books
A division of Scholastic Ltd
Euston House, 24 Eversholt Street
London, NW1 1DB, UK
Registered office: Westfield Road, Southam, Warwickshire, CV47 0RA
SCHOLASTIC and associated logos are trademarks and or registered trademarks of
Scholastic Inc.

First published in the UK by Scholastic Ltd, 2000
This edition published by Scholastic Ltd, 2008

Text copyright © Roddy Doyle, 2000
Cover illustration copyright © Charlie Fuge, 2000
Inside illustrations copyright © Brian Ajhar, 2000

The right of Roddy Doyle to be identified as the author and Brian Ajhar as the illustrator of
this work has been asserted by them.

ISBN 978 1407 10894 0

British Library Cataloguing-in-Publication Data.
A CIP catalogue record for this book is available from the British Library

Printed by CPI Bookmarque Ltd, Croydon, CR0 4TD
Papers used by Scholastic Children's Books are made from wood grown in
sustainable forests.

1 3 5 7 9 10 8 6 4 2

www.scholastic.co.uk/zone

For Kate, Jack and Rory

CHAPTER ONE

Mister Mack was walking to the train station. It was a nice, sunny morning. The birds in the trees were singing their favourite songs. And the breeze that blew was full of breakfast smells – bacon, eggs, frog's legs and cabbage.

"Yum," said Mister Mack to himself.

Mister Mack was feeling happy. Mister Mack was feeling very happy. He had a nice lunch in his lunch box – and a surprise in his flask – and his children's goodbye kisses were still tickling his cheeks. He was going to work, and he liked his job.

Actually, Mister Mack loved his job. He was a biscuit tester in a biscuit factory. It was his job to make sure that the biscuits had the right amount of chocolate, if they were supposed to have chocolate. And he measured them to make sure that they were exactly square, if they were supposed to be square, or exactly round, if they were supposed to be round. Best of all, he tasted them. Not all of them. He tasted three in the morning and four in the afternoon, to make sure that they tasted exactly right.

He was looking forward to work because, today, he was going to be testing his favourite biscuits of all time, fig-rolls. The factory made 365 types of biscuits, a different biscuit for every day of the year. Mister Mack liked most of these biscuits, and he loved some of them. But fig-rolls always came top of his list. He loved their shape. He loved their smell. He loved their intelligence. They were such clever biscuits. They were delicious without needing any help from chocolate. And today was a fig-roll-testing day. So Mister Mack was one happy man.

But on his way to the station, just after he'd turned the corner, he saw a seagull sitting on the branch of a tree.

"Do you know what, Mister?" said the seagull. "I hate fish."

"I didn't know seagulls could perch in trees," said Mister Mack.

He kept walking, but he looked back to have another look at the seagull.

And this was a pity, because he didn't see the dog poo right in front of him, on the footpath.

Poor Mister Mack.

His shoe was heading straight for that poo.

CHAPTER TWO

So what?

So what?

Yes. So what? People stand on dog poo all the time. Even dogs stand on dog poo now and again.

But it was huge. It was a big pile of wet, fresh dog poo. It was probably the biggest pile of poo in the world.

Big dog, big poo. So what? I'm bored.

I'm going to skip a few pages and see if there's any more about biscuits.

Wait. Wait! The story isn't about biscuits. And it isn't about the poo. The story is about the people who put the poo on the path so that Mister Mack would stand on it.

The people who put it there? It was dog poo, so it came out of a dog. Right?

Right.

So a dog stopped on the path outside the train station. He stayed there for a little while and left the poo before he ran away. Right?

Wrong. It was dog poo, but it wasn't a dog that put it there. And this story is about the little people who did put it there, just ten seconds before Mister Mack turned the corner.

CHAPTER THREE

Four steps, three steps, two steps.

Mister Mack had seen enough of the seagull. He was going to turn around - in plenty of time to see the poo - but the seagull spoke again.

"Fish," said the seagull. "Don't talk to me about fish."

Four steps, three steps, two steps, one.

Mister Mack's left foot was right over the dog stuff. The bottom of his shoe was exactly sixteen and a half inches from the peak of the poo.

And Mister Mack thought he heard giggles.

And he was right. He had heard giggles. Like these:

"Giggle giggle giggle."

The poo was in the middle of the path. The path was beside a garden wall. And the Gigglers were on the other side of the wall, hidden behind it.

There were three of them. They were all standing on the crossbar of a rusty old bike that had been leaning against the wall for more than twenty years. The bike was so old, it had almost become part of the wall.

The Gigglers had watched Mister Mack as he got nearer to the poo. They had counted the steps.

"How many?"

"Four."

"How many now?"

"Three."

"How many now?"

"Two."

They heard the seagull talking to Mister Mack. And they ducked behind the wall as Mister Mack walked right up to the poo.

"How many now?"

"One."

They waited.

A CHAPTER THAT ISN'T REALLY
A CHAPTER BECAUSE NOTHING REALLY
HAPPENS IN IT BUT WE'LL CALL IT
CHAPTER FOUR

Nothing happens in this chapter. But some of the questions that are probably hopping about in your heads get answered. Like this one:

Why?

Why what?

Why did the Gigglers put the poo on the path?

Good question. They did it because of

something Mister Mack had done the night before he was walking to the train station. But I'll tell you all about it later because these chapters where nothing happens get boring very quickly.

Now, back to the story.

CHAPTER FIVE
WHICH SHOULD PROBABLY BE CALLED
CHAPTER FOUR
BUT LET'S JUST CALL IT
CHAPTER FIVE

Back at the train station, the Gigglers waited.

They waited for the wallop – Mister Mack hitting the poo.

They waited for the squelch – Mister Mack stepping down on the poo.

They waited for the gasp – Mister Mack seeing the poo for the first time.

They waited for the groan – Mister Mack seeing that most of the poo was now on his shoe.

His shoe was now very, very close to the you-know-what.

"How close?" said the smallest Giggler.

"Fourteen and three-quarter inches," said the biggest Giggler.

"That's very close," said the middle-sized one.

And she shoved her fist into her mouth to trap her giggles.

And they waited.

CHAPTER SIX
WHICH SHOULD PROBABLY BE CALLED
CHAPTER FIVE
IS ANOTHER OF THESE CHAPTERS
WHERE NOTHING MUCH HAPPENS
EXCEPT FOR ONE VERY EXCITING
THING AT THE END

More questions. Like this one:

Who are the Gigglers?

Good question. The Gigglers look after children. And they do it very well. But they do it so quietly that hardly anybody has ever seen them.

How do they look after the children?

Good question. They follow them everywhere. To school, to the shops, to the park, and back home again, upstairs, into the toilet, all over the place. Everywhere the children go, the Gigglers are always near, always looking after them.

What do they look like?

Good question. Only a few people have ever seen the Gigglers and they never tell anyone else about them. So it's hard to tell what the Gigglers look like. They are baby-sized and furry. Their fur changes colour as they move.

Like a chameleon?

Yes, like a chameleon. If they are near a white wall they become white. If they are in a tree they become green and brown. If they are near a car – well, it depends on the colour of the car but they're not very good at being purple, so they try not to go too near to purple cars.

Why do they follow the children?

Another good question. They follow the children to make sure that adults are being fair to them. Parents, teachers, aunties, shopkeepers. All adults. If they are mean to the children, they get the Giggler Treatment. If they send a child to bed without their supper, or if they frighten a child, they get the Giggler Treatment. If they are dishonest to a child, if, say, they give a child fish and say it's chicken, or if they ever fart and then blame the child for it, they get the Giggler Treatment. If they are ever rude to a child or make them wear clothes that they hate, they get the Giggler Treatment.

What is the Giggler Treatment?

Poo on the shoe.

What happens then?

The adults keep getting the Treatment, every day, sometimes twice or three times a day, until they stop being mean to the child.

Have the Gigglers always done this?

Yes, since the beginning of time. The Gigglers have always been there. Since the first dog did its first poo. Since the first caveman grunted at his first cavechild. He stomped out of the cave, straight on to a huge lump of prehistoric poo.

The Roman emperor, Nero, hated children. He ordered his guards to catch all children and feed them to the lions. Then he stood on a dollop of lion poo. (There were more lions than dogs in ancient Rome.) Many years later, a saint called Patrick was busy driving all the snakes out of Ireland. A little boy called Elvis Óg O'Leary, who loved snakes, asked Patrick to stop, but Patrick pushed him out of his way – and walked straight on to a little hill of hot poo that, only seconds before, had been inside an Irish wolfhound called Bran. Saint Patrick got rid of the snakes but he never got rid of the smell.

Two minutes after the *Titanic* hit the iceberg a woman on deck shouted, "Quick, quick! The children will drown!"

"Good," said a man. "There'll be more room in the lifeboats."

And he stepped on to a hill of the slimiest green dog poo and slid off the deck, straight into the sea. "Oh Mammy!" he roared. "I forgot me water wings!"

So, you see, the Gigglers have been doing this work for thousands of years. All this time they've been giving the Treatment to men and women who are mean to children.

How was Mister Mack mean to his children?

Good question, and the answer is coming up soon. But now we'll go on to the next chapter.

What about the very exciting thing at the end of this chapter?

Oh, yes. I nearly forgot. While I was telling you all about the Gigglers, a woman who was walking in a park in Bombay nearly stood on a snail.

That wasn't exciting.

Well, the snail thought it was.

CHAPTER SEVEN
WHICH SHOULD PROBABLY BE CALLED
CHAPTER FIVE
. . . I THINK . . .
BUT LET'S JUST CALL IT . . .
I DON'T KNOW WHAT
CHAPTER IT'S SUPPOSED TO BE

The Gigglers waited. The shoe was now exactly, exactly, exactly twelve inches and a little bit from the you-know-poo.

"Any second now," whispered the biggest Giggler.

They waited for the thop thop thop – Mister Mack hopping on one foot and trying not to fall over.

They waited for the little thump – Mister Mack leaning against the wall, only three inches of brick and cement away from the Gigglers' noses.

The biggest Giggler looked over the wall, and ducked back down again. "Ten inches," she said.

"Cod?" said the seagull. "Yeuk."

The middle-sized Giggler crammed her other hand and one of her feet into her mouth, to stop the giggles from escaping. She fell off the bike but she made no noise because she landed on soft, long grass.

"Get off," said the grass.

No, it didn't. I'm only messing. But the time has come to explain why the Gigglers were doing this to Mister Mack.

CHAPTER EIGHT
WHICH SHOULD PROBABLY BE CALLED
CHAPTER . . .
HANG ON.
ONE, TWO, THREE, FOUR . . .
OH, STOP MESSING AND
GET ON WITH THE STORY

The day before Mister Mack's foot headed straight for the poo, just before it got too dark to play outside, the Mack brothers, Jimmy and Robbie, broke the kitchen window.

They were playing football with a burst ball when it happened. Robbie Mack gave the ball a whack with his big toe. It bounced off Jimmy Mack's head, flew at the window, and cracked the glass.

"Ouch!" said Robbie. "Me toe!"

"Ouch!" said Jimmy. "Me head!"

"Wah!" said Mister Mack. "Me window!"

He was upstairs when he heard the noise. He was in the bathroom, putting a plaster on his finger. He'd cut his finger putting new glass into the kitchen window, just five minutes before the ball cracked it.

He ran downstairs into the kitchen and saw the broken window. So he kept running, out to the garden. "Who did that?" he shouted.

"Not us," said Robbie. "The ball did it."

"I only just fixed it," said Mister Mack. "It's not fair."

Mister Mack had had a very hard day.

"That's seven times I've had to fix that

window," he said, "in seven days!"

He looked at Robbie and Jimmy.

"Boys, boys, boys," he said. "How many times am I going to have to fix it?"

"Eight," said Robbie.

Robbie wasn't being smart or cheeky when he said that. He was giving Mister Mack the correct answer. The window had been broken seven times, and now he was going to have to fix it once more. Seven and one made eight. So Robbie was right. But poor Mister Mack had had a very hard day. He had spent all day testing cream crackers, and they were very boring biscuits. In fact, Mister Mack didn't think that they were really biscuits at all. They were always perfectly, boringly square and they tasted like nothing except what they were, boring old cream crackers. And poor Mister Mack had been measuring and eating them all day. He was stuffed to the tonsils with cream crackers. He knew he'd dream about cream crackers tonight.

He always had the same cream cracker dream after a day of measuring and eating cream crackers. It wasn't a dream about killer ninja cream crackers or beautiful, brown-eyed cream crackers or anything interesting like that. No chance. In this dream, Mister Mack was always surrounded by talking cream crackers, hundreds of them, all saying the most boring things ever.

"Babies are smaller than adults. Isn't that interesting?"

"Toilet paper is usually white but not always. Isn't that interesting?"

"A car has four wheels but a bike has only two. Isn't that interesting?"

All night the talking cream crackers would be yapping at him. (That was another reason why Mister Mack loved fig-rolls. They never talked when he went to sleep.) He wasn't looking forward to bedtime, even though he was very tired. He could already hear the cream crackers mumbling away in his brain.

"Some pyjamas have stripes and some don't have any stripes at all. Isn't that interesting?"

But that wasn't the worst part of the day. Something strange had happened to Mister Mack at lunchtime. A vulture had swooped down from a tree and robbed his sandwiches.

And, before he'd had time to get over the shock, the vulture came back and robbed his flask. Then he'd had to fix the broken kitchen window for the seventh time in seven days, and he'd cut his finger doing it. He was hungry and tired and his finger was sore and the cream crackers were already yapping at him.

"If you put your feet in water, they get wet. Isn't that interesting?"

The vulture had stuck his tongue out at him as he flew away with the flask. The flask had been full of chicken soup, Mister Mack's all-time favourite. And now, he thought, his children were being cheeky. Mister Mack had had enough.

"Go up to your room," he told Robbie and Jimmy.

"But I'm hungry," said Jimmy.

"I don't care," said Mister Mack. "Go up to your room."

And that was why, the next morning, the poo was waiting for Mister Mack. What Mister Mack didn't know – and what nobody else knew – was that the Gigglers were listening to him. They were in the cupboard under the stairs. They looked at one another and nodded.

"The Treatment?" said the smallest, very quietly.

"The Treatment," said the biggest.

"Poo?" said the smallest.

"Poo," said the biggest.

CHAPTER SOMETHING

Back at the station, the biggest Giggler ducked back down.

"How much now?"

"Eight inches."

And the middle-sized Giggler fell off the bike again.

ANOTHER CHAPTER

Mister Mack went back into the kitchen.
The boys' mother, Billie Jean Fleetwood-
Mack, was there with the baby, Kayla.
Kayla was eating a sugar-free biscuit.

"A-bah," she said.

"No," said Billie Jean. "You can't have
one with sugar in it. They're bad for your
teeth."

"A-bah," said Kayla.

"I know you don't have any teeth," said

Billie Jean. "But you will soon."

"A-bah."

"Yes, I know your father eats biscuits. It's his job. It's dangerous work," said Billie Jean, proudly. "But somebody has to do it."

She now spoke to Mister Mack. "The boys can't go to bed without their supper," she said.

"I know," said Mister Mack. "I'll call them down in a minute."

"They didn't do it on purpose," said Billie Jean.

"I know," said Mister Mack.

"A-bah," said Kayla.

"I know," said Mister Mack.

"A-bah" was the only word that Kayla could say so far, but because all the Macks loved her so much, they always understood exactly what she meant.

Mister Mack stroked Kayla's cheek.

"It's just, it's been a hard day. You should have seen that vulture."

"A-bah?" said Kayla.

"Even bigger," said Mister Mack.

Then he went into the hall and called up the stairs. "Boys! Come down for your supper!"

"What is it?" Robbie shouted.

"Whatever you want," said Mister Mack. But the Gigglers didn't hear him this time. It was too late. They had gone. They were off looking for the good bit of poo for Mister Mack's shoe.

THE CHAPTER
AFTER THE LAST ONE

They waited for the swipe swipe swipe –
Mister Mack rubbing the shoe on some
grass.

And the chuff chuff chuff – the train
leaving, ha ha.

And the bang bang ouch – Mister Mack
banging his head off the wall.

Eight inches.

Seven.

Six.

Five.

They waited for the first big thump – Mister Mack's foot bellyflopping into the you-know-poo.

"Fish fingers?" said the seagull. "Yuk!" The middle-sized Giggler shoved her other foot into her mouth.

Why was it taking so long for Mister Mack's foot to hit the poo?

Good question. Mister Mack was wearing brand-new trousers and they were very stiff. They were so stiff, he could hardly bend and straighten his legs. Now we'll find out where the Gigglers got the you-poo-what.

THE CHAPTER BEFORE THE NEXT ONE

Dogs don't like going to the toilet on the street. But their owners make them do it.

"Come on, Rover. Let's go for a walk," says Rover's owner as he drags Rover to the front door.

"Let's go for a poo, more like," says Rover to himself. "You're not fooling me."

Poor Rover has to stand out on the street, usually late at night, in the rain and snow, thunder and lightning, in the glare of passing car lights, and go to the toilet while his owner stares straight at him.

"Good boy, Rover. Hurry up," says the owner.

"Leave me alone," says Rover to himself. "My bum is cold."

But Rover does his poo because he knows that he won't get back into the house if he doesn't.

And then the Gigglers come along.

The night that Mister Mack sent the boys up to their bedroom, Rover had done a whopper.

"Wow!" said the Gigglers, rubbing their hands and giggling. "Good old Rover. He never lets us down."

There were four Gigglers there that night. The biggest, the middle-sized, the smallest and the one that was even smaller than the smallest. This was the first time that the even smaller than the smallest Giggler had been out on a poo-finding mission, so she was very excited.

"Are we ready?" said the biggest one.

"Ready."

"Rubber gloves?"

"Rubber gloves."

"Plastic bag?"

"Plastic bag."

"Poo claw?"

"Poo claw."

The smallest Giggler lifted the poo off the path with the poo claw. This was a plastic claw like a crab's that opened and closed when she pushed a lever on its handle.

The middle-sized Giggler held the plastic bag open for the poo.

"Drop the poo," said the biggest Giggler.

"Dropping the poo," said the smallest Giggler.

And she let the poo drop into the plastic bag.

"Catching the poo," said the middle-sized Giggler.

And she closed the bag.

"Well done," said the biggest Giggler. "Twenty pence?"

"Twenty pence," said the even smaller than the smallest Giggler.

This was her big moment.

She took the money from the pouch that covered her green tummy. Her tummy was green because Rover had left the poo right beside a green car.

She held it up in the air. "Twenty pence!"

"Good," said the biggest one. "Let's go."

The money was for Rover. The Gigglers always paid for their poo.

"Rover! Rover!"

The smallest Giggler held the letter box open as the biggest one whisper-shouted into the hall of Rover's house.

Rover was upstairs sitting on the toilet. He always did this when his owner had gone to bed. His owner could never understand how the dog hair got on to the toilet seat or how the paw prints got on to the toilet paper. All dogs do this and they never, ever get caught.

"What now?" said Rover. "Can a dog have no peace?"

He wiped his bum and flushed the toilet. He washed his paws and dried them and went down to the hall. (Rover,

by the way, was the great, great, great –
keep on saying "great" for twenty minutes
– grandson of Bran, the Irish wolfhound.)

Rover saw a Giggler hand sticking
through the letter box holding a twenty-
pence piece. The door was red; the hand
was red.

He took the coin.

"Thanks, Rover," said the even smaller
than the smallest Giggler. "That was a
classic."

"Ure relcon," said Rover, because it's hard to say, "You're welcome" when you are holding a twenty-pence piece between your teeth.

Rover went into the kitchen. He found the big bone his owner had given him earlier that day. (Rover's owner, by the way, was the great, great – keep on saying "great" for two hours and thirty-seven minutes – grandson of the first caveman.) The bone was on the mat. Rover held the bone between his paws and pushed the twenty-pence piece into the hollow part where the marrow used to be.

Rover's owner loved him. He loved the way he shook himself when he was wet. He loved the way he pulled the letters through the letter box when the postman was delivering them, and he didn't mind a bit when Rover made the letters soggy. He was such a clever dog. He could beg. He could fetch sticks. What his owner didn't know – and what nobody else knew

– was that Rover was a millionaire. Rover had buried over a million pounds, all in twenty-pence pieces and all inside hollow bones, in his owner's back garden. All of that money had been given to him by the Gigglers.

"Oh, look at Rover burying the bone. Isn't he clever?"

"Ha ha ha," said Rover to himself. "You'll never know how clever."

Rover hated bones.

THIS CHAPTER
IS NAMED AFTER MY MOTHER
BECAUSE SHE SAID I COULD
STAY UP LATE IF I NAMED IT
AFTER HER
CHAPTER
MAMMY DOYLE

The biggest Giggler looked over the wall.
"Five inches," she said.

"Mackerel?" said the seagull. "Yeuk!"

THIS CHAPTER
IS NAMED AFTER
MY FRIDGE
BECAUSE IT KEEPS
ALL MY FOOD FRESH
CHAPTER FRIDGE

At the exact same time that Mister Mack was heading for the poo, Jimmy Mack fell off a stool in the kitchen as he leaned over to fill his mouth with porridge. The porridge bowl flipped over and landed on Robbie's head.

"Ouch," said Jimmy. "Me bum!"

"Ouch!" said Robbie. "Me head!"

Billie Jean came into the kitchen. She was wearing big boots and snow goggles. She had a long rope tied around her waist. She was carrying Kayla on her back and she was sweating.

Billie Jean was a mountain climber. She practised her climbing every day by running up the stairs with Kayla on her back. She did this for three hours every morning and rested only once, for five minutes, in a tent she'd pitched in the hall.

Billie Jean wanted to climb the highest mountain in every country in the world. She'd already climbed a lot of them, in Argentina, Kenya, Australia and lots of other countries.

The first mountain she'd ever climbed was in Holland. Holland is a very flat country, and its highest mountain is only ten feet high. It's so small, nobody had ever given it a name. But when Billie Jean got to the top she named it Mister Mack Mountain, after her all-time favourite husband. (Billie Jean, by the way, was the great, great – keep saying "great" for twenty minutes – granddaughter of Elvis Óg O'Leary, the little boy who tried to keep the snakes in Ireland.)

The next mountain Billie Jean was going to climb was Blue Mountain Peak in Jamaica. She was leaving the biggest one, Mount Everest in Nepal, until last. She wanted to wait until Kayla was older and then they would climb it together. Kayla was looking forward to it. All that running up the stairs on her mammy's back had given her a love of heights and adventure.

"What happened?" said Billie Jean when she saw Jimmy on the floor.

"I broke me bum," said Jimmy.

She laughed. "There's half an hour to go

before school," she said. "Why don't you go on out and play."

Jimmy forgot about his sore bum and ran out the back door.

"Bring Kayla with you," said Billie Jean.

"Okay," said Robbie as he rubbed some of the porridge off his hair with a tea towel. "Come on, Kayla."

He put Kayla on to his shoulders. "Hang on to my hair," he said.

"A-bah?" said Kayla.

"It's okay," Robbie told her. "It's only porridge."

They ran around to the front of the house and played with the burst ball.

Kayla sat on top of the wall and pretended she was on top of Mount Everest. She was a good balancer, but just to be safe, the boys stuck wet chewing gum to the wall and put her down on top of it. She was very happy up there, watching the leaves tickling one another in the tree above her and her mad brothers playing below her.

Robbie was the goalkeeper, and Jimmy kicked the ball to him. Robbie's hands missed the ball, but he caught it with his face. It bounced off his nose, hit Jimmy's elbow, and bounced again under an old oil drum.

"Ouch!" said Jimmy. "Me elbow!"

"Ouch!" said Robbie. "Me doze!"

The drum was upside down and heavy, too heavy for the boys to lift. It had been there for years, since long before the Macks had lived there. Mister Mack said that it had fallen out of the sky and that the Wicked Witch of the East was under it, but the Mack brothers weren't sure about that. Anyway, the ball was under it now.

"Now what will we do?" said Robbie.

"A-bah," said Kayla.

"Good idea, Kayla," said Robbie.

The boys ran off and got one of Billie Jean's mountain-climbing ropes from the shed. They came back and tied one end of the rope around the oil drum. Then they threw the other end up over a branch of the tree.

"Now what?" said Jimmy.

"A-bah."

"Brilliant idea."

They lifted Kayla until she held the other end of the rope. She dangled happily, but she wasn't heavy enough to budge the bin.

"A-bah," she said.

"Mega-brilliant idea."

The boys gathered some stones and put them into Kayla's nappy. She became heavier and heavier. As she dropped slowly, slowly to the ground, the bin was slowly, slowly lifted. There was soon a space big enough for Jimmy, and he crawled under the drum.

"Can you see the ball?" Robbie shouted.

"No!" Jimmy shouted back.

"Well, what can you see?"

"A monster!"

CHAPTER
TWO MILLION
AND SEVEN

"I'm not a monster," the monster said to Jimmy.

"What are you then?" said Jimmy.

"A Giggler," said the even smaller than the smallest Giggler.

Robbie grabbed Jimmy's legs and pulled him out from under the drum. And the Giggler followed Jimmy.

"Hello," she said, and she rubbed her hands and giggled. "Any second now."

"Any second now what?" said Robbie.

"Your dad's shoe will hit the poo."

"A-bah?" said Kayla.

"Rover's," said the Giggler.

And she came out from under the drum and stood up.

Hang on a minute.

How come they could see her? Aren't Gigglers supposed to be like chameleons? Aren't they able to change colour?

Good questions. Yes, they are able to change colour, but a few days before they met the even smaller than the smallest Giggler, the boys had painted the oil drum purple, and Gigglers, remember, aren't very good at being purple. So they could see her clearly. She was bright blue against the purple drum.

"A-bah?" said Kayla.

"We put it there," said the Giggler, "so your dad would walk on it."

"Why?" said Robbie.

"Because he sent you up to your room last night," said the Giggler.

"But he only sent us up for a minute," said Robbie.

"Oh-oh," said the even smaller than the smallest Giggler.

"A-bah," said Kayla.

And the Giggler agreed with her. "Yes," she said. "It is a terrible waste of poo."

Next door, Rover was burying his bone in the flower bed.

"Well, you're not getting your money back," he said to himself as he kicked muck on top of the bone.

"And it's not fair either," said Jimmy. "We'll have to warn him."

"A-bah," said Kayla.

"Good idea," said Jimmy, and he ran to get their mother, who was the fastest runner in the house.

"I've an idea," said the Giggler. "Rover!"

"Oh-oh," said Rover, in the garden beside them.

He tried to be more dog-like. He chased a fly, he scratched himself, he went woof-woof and snarled at a pair of knickers hanging on the washing line.

"Rover!"

He heard the Giggler's voice.

"Rover!"

It was a special call, like a dog whistle. Only dogs could hear a Giggler's call. And all dogs had to obey when the Giggler's called, even clever, sparky dogs like

Rover. But Rover wasn't going to give up. "Rover!"

"I can't hear you!" he shouted. "I've got a cold."

"Rover!" said the Giggler. "Jump over the wall."

"I've got a bad back."

"I'll pay you fifty pence," said the Giggler.

And Rover jumped the wall without a bother and landed right in front of the Giggler. "I take all the major credit cards," he said.

Then he saw Kayla and Robbie looking at him.

"So. I can talk," he said. "Have you got anything to say about that?"

"No," said Robbie.

"No?" said Rover. "You're not surprised? I'm a dog and I can talk."

"We know you can talk," said Robbie. "We've heard you. You're always muttering and giving out when you're digging in your garden."

"Am I?" said Rover.

"Yeah," said Robbie.

"How long have you known?" said Rover.

"A-bah," said Kayla.

"That long?" said Rover. "I'd better be more careful. The adults might hear me."

"Don't worry," said Robbie. "The adults don't listen. They just think you're barking."

He turned back to the Giggler. "So, what's the story, Gig?"

"Mister Mack's foot is heading for your poo. We have to stop him."

"My poo!" said Rover. "If he lands in it, he'll never escape. It's the best poo in the business. It's super-poo."

He ran to the wall. "Hop on, kid."

And Kayla jumped down, on to his back.

"Hang on to my ears," said Rover, and

he ran out the gate, and headed for the
train station.

The Giggler jumped on to Robbie's
back.

"Follow that baby," she said.

And Robbie ran.

Billie Jean ran out of the house with
Jimmy on her back.

"Follow that Giggler," said Jimmy.

And Billie Jean kept running.

CHAPTER SIXTEEN
(THIS CHAPTER, BY THE WAY, IS THE GREAT, GREAT, GREAT, GREAT, GREAT, GREAT, GREAT, GREAT, GREAT, GREAT, GREAT, GREAT, GREAT, GREAT GRANDSON OF CHAPTER ONE)

Back at the station, Mister Mack finally turned away from the seagull.

"Goldfish?" said the seagull. "Yeuk."

But Mister Mack wasn't interested any more. He turned his head.

In time to see the poo?

No. His foot was right over the poo now AND the poo was shaped exactly like a shoe. So Mister Mack couldn't see it.

Shoe-shaped poo. It looked exactly like the shoe's shadow. It was a trick Rover had practised over the years, and a lot of dedication and dog food had gone into getting it right.

DON'T TRY IT AT HOME, KIDS, UNLESS THERE'S AN ADULT WITH YOU.

"How much now?" said the middle-sized Giggler.

"Three inches."

"My goodness," said Mister Mack. "These are the all-time stiffest trousers I've ever worn."

And he thought he heard a dog barking.

THIS CHAPTER IS NAMED AFTER
ELVIS PRESLEY
BECAUSE HE LIVES UNDER THE SHED IN OUR BACK GARDEN

Mister Mack did hear a dog.

But it wasn't Rover.

It was just a dog.

Rover wasn't really a barking kind of dog. Actions speak louder than woofs, was Rover's motto. And, right now, Rover was probably the most active dog in the world.

He ran like the wind's big brother with Kayla, his baby jockey, on his back. He galloped so fast, his paws hardly touched the ground.

"This is cool," said his left paw, the front one.

"Good old Rover," said the right paw. "He's a flyer."

"A-bah?" said Kayla.

"Yep," said Rover. "I'm the only dog in the world with talking paws. Hang on tight."

And he galloped past the shops – the bread shop, the sweet shop, the twirly coloured pasta-that's-very-nice-with-cheese shop.

Rover was fast. And so was Robbie. Even with the Giggler on his back, he was faster than Rover, and he was catching up.

Past the bread shop, the sweetshop.

And Billie Jean was faster still. Even with Jimmy on her back and heavy mountain boots on her feet, she was zooming down the street and catching up with Robbie.

Past the twirly coloured pasta-that's-very-nice-with-cheese shop.

Rover, Robbie and Billie Jean – they were the fastest things on eight feet.

But would they be quick enough?

A VERY SHORT
CHAPTER
TO LET YOU KNOW HOW MANY INCHES
MISTER MACK'S FOOT WAS
AWAY FROM THE POO

Two.

THERE IS MORE THAN ONE SIDE TO EVERY STORY, AND THIS STORY HAS LOTS OF SIDES:
THE CREAM CRACKERS GIVE THEIR SIDE OF THE STORY

We weren't there. We saw nothing. Isn't that interesting?

A REAL CHAPTER

Rover ran.

The clothes shop, the toy shop, the colouring pencil shop.

As he ran past the pet shop he looked at the doggies in the window. "So long, suckers!" he shouted.

The shoe shop, the sock shop, the grandfather clock shop.

Robbie and Billie Jean caught up with him.

"Do you know any good shortcuts, Rover?" said Robbie.

"Woof," said Rover.

He wasn't going to talk in front of an adult, he didn't care how nice she was.

ROVER
GIVES HIS SIDE
OF THE STORY

Shhhhh.

I have to be very quiet. If my owner wakes up and catches me typing on his computer, I'll have a lot of explaining to do. I can just hear him:

"How did Rover plug it in?"

"Just what exactly was Rover doing in here?"

"How did Rover know how to spell his name?"

He nearly caught me last week. I was sending an e-mail to my girlfriend in Galway. Her family moved there a few months ago, and I've a feeling I miss her more than she misses me. Anyway, there I am, writing her a love poem, trying to think of a good word to rhyme with "Lassie" – that's her name, by the way – when I hear the owner turning on the bedside light. I was out of here and downstairs on my mat before his feet hit the floor. Then he must have noticed that the computer was on. And do you know what he said?

"Who put the paw marks on the mouse?"

Can you believe that? Who lives here, for Dog's sake? The owner, his wife, four big kids, and one dog. The owner, his wife, and the four big kids have hands and feet, and the one dog has paws.

"Who put the paw marks on the mouse?" the man asks.

Anyway, I still have to be careful, even if my owner isn't exactly a master detective.

There's only one thing I want to say. If I had known that the Gigglers were going to use my poo on the Mack guy's shoe I would never have sold it to them. I swear to Dog, I would never have done it. I have to make a living and I like what the Gigglers do – I like their style. But I've seen the Mack guy playing with his kids. He's a good father, a loving husband, all that corny stuff. He brings biscuits home from work and he often throws a few over the wall to good old Rover. Okay, they're not exactly fresh, but it's the thought that counts.

I like the guy. And I'll say this: if Rover likes a guy, he doesn't go around pooing on his shoe.

Anyway, that's all I wanted to say. I'd better get out of here. The owner is mumbling in his sleep. That means he's going to get up for a pee or a sandwich.

I'm out of here. Double click.

HOW MANY
INCHES NOW?

One.

Just one inch. The sole of Mister Mack's shoe was an inch – less than an inch – from the tip of the poo.

Where were Rover and Kayla? Where were Robbie and the even smaller than the smallest Giggler? Where were Billie Jean and Jimmy?

Two-thirds of an inch.

Half an inch.

Less than half an inch.

Where were they?

WELL,
WHERE WERE THEY?

Rover knew a shortcut. Rover knew every shortcut in town. Rover knew every short-cut in the world.

Rover ran, and the others followed him. He ran down a lane beside the cake shop. At the end of the lane, a wall – Rover jumped – and at the other side, a small river –

"Hang on, kid."

Rover jumped.

His back paws touched the water, his

nails scratched the riverbank, mud and stones fell back into the river. But Rover had made it across.

"A-bah," said Kayla.

"Thanks, toots," said Rover.

He kept running.

Robbie jumped but he was going to fall into the river – he hadn't jumped far enough. He held his nose and got ready for the splash, when Billie Jean, in mid-air, grabbed the back of Robbie's shirt and continued on her jump across the river.

They all landed in a big heap on the other bank.

"Isn't this great fun?" said Billie Jean.

"Don't forget the poo, Mum," said Jimmy.

"Oh, yes," said Billie Jean.

And they were off again, after Rover and Kayla.

HOW FAR NOW?

Less than less than half an inch.

The Gigglers behind the wall got their ears ready. Oh, they loved that sweet sound. The glorious squelch of an adult foot sinking into the best poo that money could buy. It was music to their furry ears.

Mister Mack could hear the train coming.

KAYLA
GIVES HER SIDE
OF THE STORY

A-bah.
  A-bah, a-bah.
  A-bah, a-bah, a-bah.
  A-bah.
  A-bah, a-bah, a-bah, a-bah, a-bah.
  A-bah.
  A-bah, a-bah, a-bah –
  A-bah.

JIMMY AND ROBBIE
GIVE THEIR SIDE
OF THE STORY

JIMMY: We think it's a brilliant idea.

ROBBIE: Yes, we do.

JIMMY: Giving adults the Giggler Treatment.

ROBBIE: Making them walk on poo.

JIMMY: It's fair and it's funny.

ROBBIE: It's very funny.

JIMMY: But if we'd known that the

Gigglers were going to give our daddy the Treatment –

ROBBIE: If we'd known –

JIMMY: I think we would have tried to stop them sooner.

ROBBIE: We probably would have.

JIMMY: Even though it's funny.

ROBBIE: Even though it's brilliant.

JIMMY: It's the funniest thing ever.

ROBBIE: Funnier even than doing rudies in the bath.

ROBBIE: We probably would have warned him.

JIMMY: Probably.

ROBBIE: Even though the ball broke the window, not us.

JIMMY: And even though he wouldn't let me put one of Kayla's nappies in the toaster to see what would happen.

ROBBIE: And even though he wouldn't let me make a kite out of Granny's knickers, and she wasn't even wearing them.

JIMMY: And even though he wouldn't

let me pick my nose, even though there was a brilliant bit of snot up there and I wanted to flick it at Grandad because he was asleep and his mouth was open.

ROBBIE: And even though he wouldn't let me slide off the roof with Kayla on my head.

JIMMY: We would probably have tried to stop the Gigglers sooner.

ROBBIE: Even though it was really funny.

JIMMY: Really, really funny.

WHAT'S KEEPING ROVER?

Rover ran across a field. He ran across a road. He ran across the Sahara Desert.

"A-bah?" said Kayla.

"Yeah, kid," said Rover. "It's the Sahara. Trust me."

Billie Jean caught up with Rover. "Are you sure this is the way?"

"Woof," said Rover.

Robbie caught up with them. "We never went this way to the station before," he said.

"Woof," said Rover.

They climbed over a huge sand dune, and there in front of them, was a huge, wide river.

"Oh my goodness," said Billie Jean. "It's the river Nile."

"Cool," said Jimmy.

"Lift your legs, kid," Rover whispered to Kayla.

And he ran into the water, and swam when it got too deep for his legs. Robbie followed Rover. He was an excellent swimmer, even with the Giggler on his back. And Billie Jean followed Robbie. She couldn't swim but Jimmy could, so she held on to his trousers.

Rover swam across the river. "See that log, kid?" he said.

"A-bah."

"Well, it's a crocodile," said Rover.

It was a crocodile. It was a vegetarian crocodile, the only veggie croc in the river that day.

"Bet you wish I was a carrot," Rover said
to the croc as they swam past him.

They swam to the far side and climbed
the sandy bank.

"Not far now, kid," said Rover.

NOT FAR!!

Measure a mouse's eyelash. Not down. Across. That was how far Mister Mack's shoe was from the poo.

And his rescuers were in Egypt!

In North Africa!

They'd never make it on time.

WHERE IN THE WORLD IS ROVER?

Rover climbed the steep, sandy bank of the river Nile – and saw, right in front of him, the Eiffel Tower.

"Yes!" said Rover. "Ha, ha. Just as I expected."

He ran.

THE SEAGULL
GIVES HIS SIDE
OF THE STORY

Fish?
  Fish?
  Don't talk to me about fish.
  I hate fish.
  Cod?
  Yeuk.
  Salmon?
  Yeuk.

Jellyfish?

Yeuk.

Herring, haddock, halibut?

Yeuk, yeuk, yeuk.

Fish fingers?

Yeuk.

Fish toes? Fish necks, elbows, knees, eyes, fish teeth, fish hair, fish glasses?

Yeuk, yeuk, yeuk for a million years.

Fish?

If I had my way I'd round them all up and throw them into the sea.

WHERE IN
THE WORLD
IS ROVER?
(II)

Rover ran to the Eiffel Tower, through the tourists and ice-cream sellers.

A man with a flowery shirt and a video camera stood in his way.

"What's the matter, pal?" said Rover as he ran between the man's legs. "Did you never see a baby on a dog's back before?" The man's mouth dropped open.

"Did that dog just talk?" he asked his wife, whose mouth had also dropped open.

"I . . . think . . . so?" she said.

"How come he didn't speak French?" said the man.

"Maybe he's on his holiday, too," said the woman.

"Ah," said the man. "That explains it."

Under the Eiffel Tower, beside one of the giant metal legs that lifted the tower to the sky, Rover found what he was looking for. It was a rabbit hole, hidden under a bush, and Rover dived into it.

He ran through the dark of the tunnel. They could hear the others behind them. They ran and they ran.

Then they saw it – a tiny dot of light in front of them.

They ran and they ran, and the dot got bigger and bigger, but it was still very small, still far away. They ran and they ran and now the dot was getting bigger and much brighter.

Rover was getting tired. He was panting and thirsty.

He took one last breath, and ran – and jumped into the bright, bright light – and landed in the garden, right behind the Gigglers on the bike.

"Mind the poo!" he shouted.

Kayla flew off Rover's back, over the bike and the Gigglers' heads, right over the wall and landed in her father's arms.

"A-bah!"

Mister Mack looked down.

Too late.

His foot was in the poo. The left leg of his brand-new trousers was up to its knee in Rover's –

"Stop right there."

Yes, Rover?

"Are you saying that I was too late?"

Yes, Rover.

"Are you seriously saying that I was too late? After all that? The Mack guy's foot ends up in the stink?"

Yes, Rover. You see, it's funnier if Mister Mack's shoe –

"Forget funnier, pal. And listen. See these teeth?"

Yes, Rover.

"Now they're funny. See your ankle?"

Yes, Rover.

"My teeth get to know your ankle. Now that's what I call funny. Ha, ha, ha. Do you understand me, pal?"

Yes, Rover.

"Well, then. Was Rover too late?"

No, Rover.

"Good. We'll start again."

Yes, Rover.

ROVER
SAVES THE DAY

Rover was getting tired. He was panting and thirsty. But brave Rover kept running. He took one last breath – and brave, handsome Rover jumped into the bright, bright light – and landed in the garden, right behind the Gigglers on the bike.

"Mind the poo!" he shouted.

Kayla flew off Rover's back, over the bike and the Gigglers' heads, right over the wall and landed in her father's arms.

"A-bah!"

Mister Mack looked down.

Just in time.

His shoe was right there, right bang on top of the poo. How near? How close? The shoe was kissing the poo.

Mister lifted his foot and walked right over the poo.

And now, Rover jumped over the wall. Followed by Robbie and the even smaller than the smallest Giggler.

Followed by Jimmy and Billie Jean.

Followed by the other three Gigglers, biggest, middle-sized and smallest.

Hang on a minute.

How come they could see the Gigglers?

When they want to be seen, the Gigglers can be seen. They stopped being grey, the colour of the wall, and became bright blue in exactly three seconds.

Billie Jean looked at the poo and at Mister Mack's shoe. "Oh, thank goodness, you're safe," she said.

"Yes," said Mister Mack. "But if it hadn't

been for. . . Hang on," said Mister Mack. "You did say, 'Mind the poo.'"

"A-bah," said Kayla.

"You, Kayla?" said Mister Mack. "Your first words! 'Mind the poo!' This is the happiest day of my life. Say it again, Kayla. Say, 'Mind the poo.'"

"A-bah," said Kayla.

"She said it again!" said Mister Mack.

He kissed her forehead. He held her over his head. He laughed.

"For a minute there I thought it was the dog that said it."

"Woof," said Rover.

"Dogs can't talk, Dad," said Jimmy.

"Woof," said Rover.

"Who ever heard of a dog talking?" said Robbie.

"Take it easy, pal," Rover whispered. "You're overdoing it."

The biggest Giggler came up to Mister Mack.

"Sorry about the poo," she said.

"What about the poo?" said Mister Mack.

She explained about adults being mean to children, and dog poo, and Rover, and plastic bags and shoes.

"But we made a mistake with you," she said.

"That's okay," said Mister Mack. "Keep up the good work. The vulture doesn't work for you, does he?"

"No," said the smallest Giggler. "But we know him. He doesn't really like being a vulture. He much prefers sandwiches to dead bodies."

"I'll share mine with him," said Mister Mack. "But not today."

Mister Mack had a trick up his sleeve. Well, actually, it wasn't up his sleeve. It was in his flask. He had filled the flask with orange juice, with "bits". And, as everybody knows, vultures don't like "bits". He was looking forward to lunchtime but he said nothing to the Gigglers.

"Would you all like to come back to our house for breakfast?" said Billie Jean.

"We'd love to," said the biggest Giggler. "But there's a woman waiting for the Giggler Treatment. She wouldn't let her kids watch telly because they didn't finish their parsnips."

"Oh, the mean old thing," said Billie Jean.

"She'll be walking to the train station in a few minutes," said the biggest Giggler. "We need some of the fresh stuff. Rover?"

The middle-sized Giggler handed a twenty-pence piece to Rover.

"Put your money back in your pouch, pal," said Rover, very quietly. "This one's on me."

He walked past Kayla.

"It's a dog's life," he whispered. "Bye bye, kid."

And he walked behind a bush, humming a song called "How Much Is That Human in the Window?"

The middle-sized Giggler followed him with a plastic bag. The smallest Giggler followed with her poo claw. And the even smaller than the smallest Giggler followed them and, as they walked away, they became green like the bush, and disappeared.

Then Mister Mack heard the train leaving the station. "Oh no," he said. "I'm going to be late for work. The fig-rolls will be all gone. I'll be tasting cream crackers again. All day."

He could already hear them.

"When grass gets long, you cut it with a lawn mower. Isn't that interesting?"

"If you close your eyes, you can't see. Isn't that interesting?"

But Kayla saved the day again. "A-bah," she said.

"Chocolate-covered cream crackers!" said Mister Mack. "What a brilliant idea! Thanks, Kayla."

"Fish-covered cream crackers?" said the seagull.

He flew off his branch.

"I'm going back to the sea," he said. "Well away from fish."

But Mister Mack didn't hear him. He was running to the train station. He could already taste the new, exciting, chocolate cream crackers. He could already hear them.

"In 1984, a man ate thirteen raw eggs in one second. Isn't that interesting?"

"A man once pulled two train carriages with his teeth. Isn't that interesting?"

Mister Mack was one happy man.

A CHAPTER
THAT ISN'T REALLY
A CHAPTER
BECAUSE THE STORY ENDED
AT THE END OF THE
LAST CHAPTER

All good stories have messages, and this story has loads of them. Here are some of them:

1. If a vulture ever robs your sandwiches, remember, he's only doing it because he doesn't want to eat you. (The vulture, by the way, was the great, great –

keep saying great for two hours and twenty-seven minutes – grandson of the pterodactyl that pooed on the first caveman's head the day after he stepped on the first prehistoric dog poo.)

2. Something else.

3. Your dog might not talk to you, but that doesn't mean that he or she can't talk. Also, not all dogs are millionaires, only the ones that poo a lot.

4. The seagull – make one up yourself.

5. If you have a baby like Kayla Mack in your house, always listen to her advice, especially if it has anything to do with chocolate and cream crackers.

6. And last, if you are an adult and you ever walk on dog poo, ask yourself, "Why are the Gigglers giving me the Giggler Treatment?" But remember, it might not be the Giggler Treatment. It might just be poo.

THE END

"Hey, pal."

Oh, yes. Sorry, Rover. I nearly forgot.

7. If your name is Lassie and you live in Galway, Rover says hi.

THE END

Look out for Roddy Doyle's next fantastic children's book:

ROVER SAVES CHRISTMAS

Jimmy and Robbie Mack were very excited and very bored. It was Christmas Eve and they wanted the day to end, so they could go to bed and wake up the next morning.

Christmas Day.

The best day in the whole year.

They'd been thinking about nothing else for months.

"What do you want for breakfast?" their mother had asked Jimmy last October.

"Christmas," said Jimmy.

"What is the capital of France?" their teacher, Mister Eejit, had asked on the last day before the holidays.

"Presents," said Robbie.

Robbie and Jimmy been extra-specially good for the last few weeks.

For example, they had helped their Granda to find his false teeth. They were super-glued to the roof of his car. (Jimmy and Robbie had glued the teeth to the roof but it is much more important to know that they had helped poor old Granda to find them. And, by the way, they got the teeth off the roof with a can opener.) They'd spent all their pocket-money on presents for the people they loved – *Banjo-Kazooie* for their mother, a new uniform for Granny's Action Man, a special pair of scissors for their father, for cutting the horrible big hairs that grew out of his ears and nose, a T-shirt with "Barney Smokes Big Fat Cigars" on it for their baby sister, and a brand new can opener for Granda. (The old one was stuck in the roof of his car.)

They had tied their stockings to the ends of their beds. They had made twenty-seven cheese sandwiches and left them in a huge pile on the mantelpiece for Santa. They had cut the crusts off the sandwiches because Santa never ate the crusts. And they had left one of their mother's cans of Guinness on the mantelpiece beside the sandwiches, and a carrot for Rudolf.

But there were still hours and hours to go before bedtime.

"How long now?" said Jimmy.

"Thirteen hours and thirty-seven minutes," said Robbie.

"I think I'll make another sandwich for Santa."

"I think I'll peel Rudolf's carrot."

The brothers were walking to the back door. They were soaking wet and hungry and excited and bored and their little sister jumped out of an upstairs window of the house next-door.